ASTRID SHECKELS
Nic and Nellie

Islandport Press
P.O. Box 10
Yarmouth, Maine 04096
books@islandportpress.com
www.islandportpress.com

Production Date: April, 2013
Plant & Location: Printed by Tara TPS, Seoul, South Korea
Job/Batch #: 120790

ISBN: 978-1-934031-52-0
Library of Congress Control Number: 2012945245
Dean L. Lunt, publisher
Book design, Karen Hoots

ISLANDPORT PRESS YARMOUTH • MAINE

For Katrine

Nic and her dog, Nellie, were set to spend the entire summer with Grandma and Grandpa on the island. Nic had visited before, but never for so long, and never without her parents and sisters. This was going to be her very own grand adventure. Nic couldn't wait!

But now that she was actually on the island—alone—she suddenly felt very nervous. Maybe she wasn't so big and brave after all? Maybe she should just go back home where she had friends.

"Have fun!" Mom said, hugging Nic good-bye. Nic didn't say a word. She just held on very, very, very tightly to Nellie's leash.

Nic lugged her backpack up to her summer bedroom. She was staying in her mom's childhood room, which still had some of her mom's old things laying around. Nic touched the faded face of a doll, a worn book cover, and seashells, but they made her homesick. In the past, Nic had shared this room with her sisters, and it felt very lonely without them. She curled up on the bed clutching her special stuffed raccoon. Nellie rested her head on Nic's feet.

After lunch, Grandma gave Nic a great, big island hug.

"Why don't you take a walk out to the back beach, Nicola?" Grandma asked. Nic's real name was Nicola, but everyone called her Nic, except Grandma.

"I don't know," Nic said hesitantly.

"No, no, it will be fun. Run along and I'll see you later."

Nic knew that the back beach was Mom's favorite island spot. It was filled with smooth rocks and pebbles. Nic listened to the swish of the long grass against her legs as she and Nellie trudged through it. She saw grasshoppers leap and heard the distant clanging of a bell buoy. She breathed deep the wonderful smell of spruce trees.

Nic rolled a beach stone in her hands. The rock was so smooth and so round and so pretty. The ocean had rolled it against other rocks, wearing down every bump and rough edge. Mom said that holding an island rock in her hands always made her feel like she was home. Nic filled her pockets with rocks.

That night, she tossed and turned in the dark room. She tightly clutched her raccoon and a beach rock, but a tear still slipped down her cheek.

Nic woke up early the next morning when Nellie jumped on her bed, ready to start a new day. She sleepily followed her dog to the front porch where Grandpa sat drinking coffee.

"Good morning, Grandpa," said Nic as she sat down beside him.

"Good morning, Nic," said Grandpa. "You know, I just love an early morning sunrise, all golden and new. I imagine that this island is the first place touched by the sun's rays. It reminds me that each day promises new adventures."

Nic scooted closer to him. She wasn't so sure.

Nic and Nellie went with Grandma to pick blueberries so they could make one of Grandma's delicious blueberry pies. Nic tried to help by filling her own bucket, but she ended up eating most of what she had picked. Nellie spilled the rest.

After a while, Grandma stopped picking and just listened.

"I love to hear the wind sighing in the tall trees," Grandma said softly. Nic listened too. She liked the sound.

Later, Nic and Nellie wandered out to Gray Rock Ledge. Nic named one enormous rock "The Elephant," but then decided it would be more fun as a giant sailing ship. Nic perched on top, a famous explorer gazing out at an island she had just discovered. Nellie, her loyal first mate, sat beside her, watching for danger as seagulls soared in the sky above.

That night, after supper and blueberry pie, Nic went to bed. She lay awake, wide-eyed, thinking and thinking and thinking. She still clutched a beach rock and her raccoon, but this time she did not cry.

After supper the next day, Nic's older cousin Kate took Nic to the island store for ice cream. The small shop sold bread, milk, postcards, and penny candy. It was also the island's post office. Nic chose her favorite—strawberry ice cream in a cone. Kate ordered mint chocolate chip. The girls ate their ice cream outside on the steps. Nellie seemed to like Kate's best.

FROZEN YOGURT

ICE CREAM

One morning, Nic and Nellie wandered down to the wharf. The harbor was noisy with men's voices, boat engines, and screeching gulls. Nic soon spotted Rosie feeding ducks. Together, they tossed bread crusts into the water.

"I just love the ducks," said Rosie.

"Me too," said Nic.

Rosie gave Nellie a piece of bread to eat. Nellie wagged her tail for more.

Later, Nic and Nellie and Rosie discovered Clint poking sticks into the smelly mudflats.
"Yuck, this mud stinks!" said Nic as she gingerly tiptoed out into the squishy mud toward the boy.

"What? It smells great!" Clint said. "I love mud!"

Nic did like the feel of mud oozing between her toes and she liked getting dirty, but she wasn't sure she liked the smell. Nellie didn't seem to mind.

Back at the wharf, Nic and Nellie and Rosie met Jed, who took them for
a tour of the harbor in his old rowboat. They mostly paddled around in
big circles because one of the oars was broken. Nic laughed as Jed told
thrilling stories about pirates on the high seas and buried treasure.
There was danger everywhere!

One sunny afternoon, Jed, Clint, Rosie, and another girl, Emily, took Nic and Nellie to the salt ponds for a picnic. Grandma packed Nic a ham-and-cheese sandwich and fresh blueberries for lunch. Jed taught Nic how to skip flat rocks across the water. The ponds weren't very deep, but Nellie made sure that everyone got thoroughly wet.

"Yo ho ho!" Jed laughed like a pirate. Jed really loved pirates. So did Nic.

That evening, Grandpa and Kate made a fire on the rocky beach. Nic and the other island kids roasted hot dogs and bread dough and marshmallows. As the fire flickered and sparked, Nic listened to frogs in the nearby bog and the clanging of a bell buoy. She caught a whiff of mud. She remembered the taste of wild blueberries. She watched her new friends laughing.

She smiled a big, wide smile and hugged Nellie tight. She couldn't even remember being sad!

Nic and Nellie woke early the next morning to watch another island sunrise with Grandpa.

Grandpa could see some caked mud on Nic's toes and some marshmallow stuck in her hair. He laughed. "I think you're becoming a real island girl," he told Nic. "You're right at home!"

"Nellie and I love it here," she answered. "And I want to come back every summer. Just me and Nellie."

Grandpa laughed again as Nic gave him a great, big island hug.

ght

What is quite bright at the park tonight?

(lights)

night
lighthouse
knight
eight

24